The *very* Fairy Princess

Valentines from the Heart

by **Julie Andrews** *&* **Emma Walton Hamilton**

Illustrated by **Christine Davenier**

LITTLE, BROWN & COMPANY

LB kids

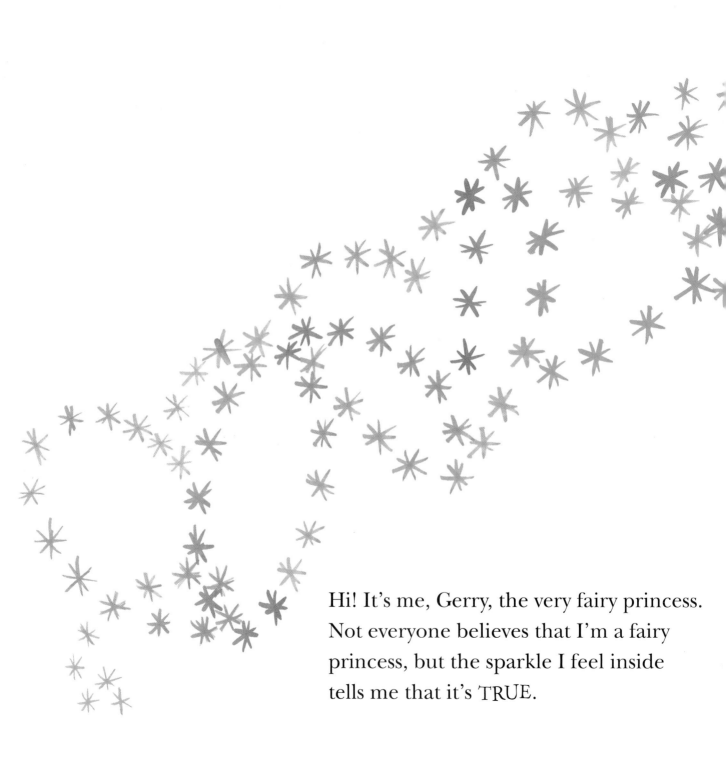

Hi! It's me, Gerry, the very fairy princess. Not everyone believes that I'm a fairy princess, but the sparkle I feel inside tells me that it's TRUE.

One of my FAVORITE days is coming up—Valentine's Day! Fairy princesses are at their sparkly best making people smile, and what better way to do that than with a FABULOUS homemade card?

I use TONS of glitter, sequins, and feathers,
as well as stickers, doilies, buttons, crystals, ribbons,
and ANYTHING that catches my fancy.
(I find it helps to sing while I'm working.)

I make valentines for everybody in my family,
and each one of my friends at school.
It's kind of hard to make one for Connor,
because he likes bugs and pulls my hair in class,
but I do my best.
(Fairy princesses are EXTREMELY gracious.)

Mommy gives me one of Daddy's folders, to keep my cards safe.

On Valentine's Day morning, Daddy makes heart-shaped
pancakes with extra fairy dust on top. YUM!
I give Mommy, Daddy, and Stewart their valentines.
Mommy's is covered with sequined flowers,
because she likes to garden.

Daddy loves to cook, so his has a crystal cake.
Stewart's has a trumpet
made of buttons and string.
Look—here's one for me,
with a sparkly pop-up fairy inside! PERFECT!

Now it's time to get ready for school—
our class is having a Valentine's Day party!
I put on my BEST tiara and wings for the occasion.

I also try to find all my heart-shaped accessories,
but it's been a year since I last wore them,
so they're all in different places.
(Fairy princesses are busy, so they sometimes
forget to tidy their rooms.)

Finally, I'm ready—but now I'm late for school!
Stewart is already halfway down the block.
Daddy hands me my lunch, and Mommy gives me my backpack.

But wait! Where are my valentines?
I rush back inside and grab the folder.
I practically FLY to make it to the bus on time!

At school, everyone is excited.
Miss Pym has done WONDERS with the classroom!
We each get a bag with our name on it for collecting cards.

I can hardly wait!
(Fairy princesses LOVE giving surprises!)

I hug my special folder,

then open it carefully.

But what's this?
These aren't my valentines!
These are Daddy's work papers!

My day is RUINED!
This is going to be the most
UN-sparkly day in valentine history!

Miss Pym gives me a hug and says not to worry.
"But I worked on them for weeks! I made something special for
everybody. . . . In yours, I told you what a great teacher you are!"
"Well, thank you!" She smiles. "You just told me again."

I blink very hard, trying not to cry.
(Fairy princesses must maintain
their composure, especially in public.)

Suddenly, I have an idea.

I whisper to Miss Pym and she nods enthusiastically.

Clapping her hands, she says to the class,

"One, two, three, eyes on me!

We have a small problem. Gerry's cards have been misplaced.

So she'd like to give you each a *different* kind of valentine.

Please join us on the rug."

Everyone sits in a circle.
I stand in front of Delilah and take a deep breath.

"I love it when you play the trombone," I tell her. "It REALLY makes you sparkle!" She looks happy, and her face turns a little pink.

One by one, I tell ALL my friends what I love best about each of them.

I tell José he sparkles
on his skateboard.

Cody Rose sparkles
when she reads out loud,

and Patrick's teeth sparkle when he smiles.
(Fairy princesses are very attentive to details.)

Finally, I get to Connor.
What can I say?
"You sparkle when you . . ."
I bite my lip.

". . . RESCUE bugs! And you're EXTREMELY enthusiastic."
(Whewwww! Fairy princesses always come through in a pinch.)

Suddenly the classroom door opens.
It's DADDY!
"I think we had a folder mix-up this morning,"
he says, grinning. "Is this one yours, Princess?"
MY VALENTINES!

I rush over, and he lifts me in the air.
Everyone cheers!

Miss Pym invites Daddy to join us for pink lemonade and cupcakes
with hearts on them. We open all our cards and have a GREAT party.
"This was a blast!" Connor says. "But the best part was
when Gerry TOLD us our valentines. She sparkles ALL THE TIME!"

Now I'M the one who's turning pink. . . .
But maybe that's the perfect color for a very fairy princess on
Valentine's Day!

Pour Christine, qui nous adorons, et qui rend notre Gerry plus
étincelant que nous l'imaginions.
—J.A. & E.W.H.

Pour Delphine, ma petite cousine chérie qui doit suivre
son coeur pour trouver le bonheur!
—C.D.

The illustrations for this book were done in ink and color pencil on Kaecolor paper.
The text was set in Baskerville and the display type is Mayfair.